HAUNTED PLACES

HAUNTED PRISONS

KENNY ABDO

Fly!
An Imprint of Abdo Zoom
abdobooks.com

abdobooks.com

Published by Abdo Zoom, a division of ABDO, P.O. Box 398166, Minneapolis, Minnesota 55439. Copyright © 2021 by Abdo Consulting Group, Inc. International copyrights reserved in all countries. No part of this book may be reproduced in any form without written permission from the publisher. Fly!™ is a trademark and logo of Abdo Zoom.

Printed in the United States of America, North Mankato, Minnesota.
052020
092020

Photo Credits: AP Images, Granger Collection, iStock, newscom, North Wind Picture Archives, Shutterstock, ©HelenOnline p14 / CC BY-SA 3.0
Production Contributors: Kenny Abdo, Jennie Forsberg, Grace Hansen
Design Contributors: Dorothy Toth, Neil Klinepier

Library of Congress Control Number: 2019956179

Publisher's Cataloging-in-Publication Data

Names: Abdo, Kenny, author.
Title: Haunted prisons / by Kenny Abdo
Description: Minneapolis, Minnesota : Abdo Zoom, 2021 | Series: Haunted places | Includes online resources and index.
Identifiers: ISBN 9781098221331 (lib. bdg.) | ISBN 9781644944141 (pbk.) | ISBN 9781098222314 (ebook) | ISBN 9781098222802 (Read-to-Me ebook)
Subjects: LCSH: Haunted places--Juvenile literature. | Haunted prisons--Juvenile literature. | Ghosts--Juvenile literature.
Classification: DDC 133.122--dc23

TABLE OF CONTENTS

Prisons............................ 4

The History 8

The Haunted 12

The Media 20

Glossary 22

Online Resources 23

Index 24

PRISONS

The world's worst and most sinister criminals have been held in prisons. Some say their **spirits** are still trapped behind bars to this day.

Abandoned prisons have gone down in history as some of the most haunted places in the world.

THE HISTORY

Prisons have existed since the creation of societies. Once societies set up the written word, they were able to create a **code of law** for people to live by. If those were broken, you would be punished.

Prisons grew and evolved throughout the centuries. From simple jails to sprawling penitentiaries, they were always known more for their cruelty than their **reformation**.

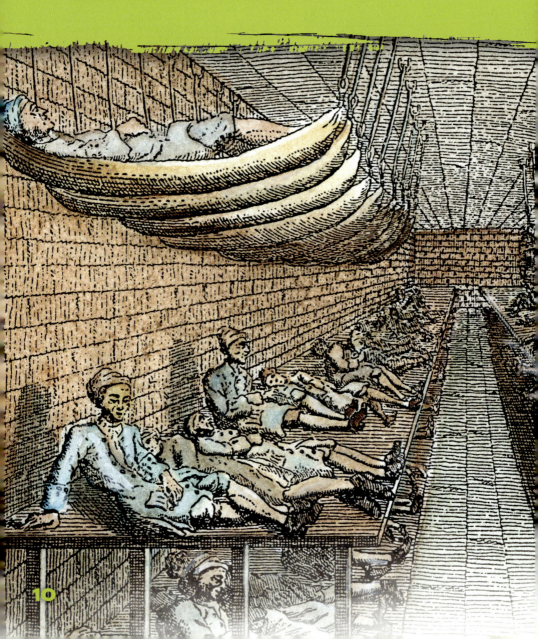

Today, abandoned prisons around the world hold a dark history within their evil cells.

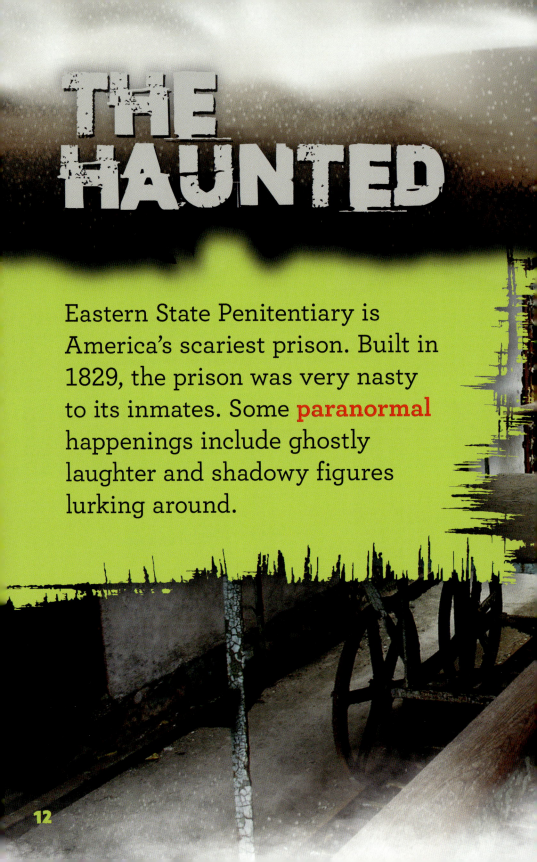

THE HAUNTED

Eastern State Penitentiary is America's scariest prison. Built in 1829, the prison was very nasty to its inmates. Some **paranormal** happenings include ghostly laughter and shadowy figures lurking around.

The Castle of Good Hope was a **refill station** in Cape Town. It changed into a prison in 1899. People have seen the ghosts of **executed** prisoners. The bell tower still rings even though it's been sealed up for centuries.

West Virginia Penitentiary is one of the most haunted prisons in the United States. Former guards saw ghosts of past inmates, including one they called the "shadow man," and have heard and felt unexplained things.

Bodmin Jail in England was built by prisoners of war in 1779. It hosted more than 50 public hangings of inmates. Some of whom still hang around to this day.

The Tower of London is a disturbing tourist stop in the United Kingdom. It was built in 1066 by William the Conqueror. It was a prison and **execution** site for peasants and royals alike. Today, Catherine Howard, wife to Henry VIII, can be seen running through the **gallery**, screaming for help.

Alcatraz prison has some of the most **paranormal** activity in the world. You can hear cries and moans that belong to no one.

Cellblock C is haunted by the **spirit** of Abie Maldowitz, or the Butcher, as he was known by the guards and other inmates.

THE MEDIA

Ghost hunters have explored the spookiest prisons. Several hauntings have been documented in movies, books, and TV shows.

People should avoid going to prison. They might have to bunk-up with ghosts still serving their afterlife **sentences**.

GLOSSARY

code of law – a written down system of laws to be obeyed for particular areas.

execute – to put to death by law.

gallery – an area of a building that is usually long, narrow, and has a certain function.

paranormal – an occurrence beyond the scope of scientific understanding.

refill station – a post that ships could sail up to and replenish any needs.

reformation – the practice of improving a person to reenter society.

sentences – to be confined in a prison for a set amount of time if found guilty of a crime.

spirit – a being that is not of this world, such as a ghost. Some believe that a spirit is a force that is a part of humans that lives on after they die.

ONLINE RESOURCES

To learn more about haunted prisons, please visit **abdobooklinks.com** or scan this QR code. These links are routinely monitored and updated to provide the most current information available.

Alcatraz Prison 18, 19

Eastern State Penitentiary 12

England 16, 17

Henry VIII 17

Howard, Catherine 17

laws 8

Maldowitz, Abie 19

media 20

South Africa 14

types 10

West Virginia 15

West Virginia Penitentiary 15

William the Conqueror 17